THE ANGEL and the JUDGMENT

The Preacher

The Angel

The Narrator

The Young Man

The Newscasters

The preacher thundered in a powerful surge of

The Judgment Is Coming!

"IN JESUS' NAME!"

faith. His hand lay heavily on the brow of a weeping

and hopeful saint.

"IN JESUS' NAME!"

His voice again thundered throughout the packed

auditorium. Hundreds watched as the man of God

concentrated his prayers on the needs before him. A

whimpering voice was barely audible over the loud-

speakers.

The Angel and the Judgment

1

The Judgment Is Coming'

ISBN 1-56043-154-7 © Copyright 1996 — Don Nori

Tears streamed down the young man's face as a

The Judgment Is Coming.

"Nothing happened. Nothing happened. I did everything you told me to do, but nothing happened."

sense of utter hopelessness filled his heart. He looked

up at the man of God in anticipation of help and guidance.

"Do you believe the Word of God?"
came the challenging voice of the preacher.

"Yes, yes I do, but nothing is happening and...and I really do not think that anything is going to happen,"
the young man sheepishly confessed.

"What did God say?"
was the nearly mocking reply from the man of God.

The Angel and the Judgment   3   The Judgment Is Coming!

The preacher turned a pitiful gaze on the young man,

The Judgment Is Coming!

"I...I know what God said, er, I know what you said, and I don't know if..."

"Thank You, Jesus! Thank You, Lord! You have revealed a spirit of unbelief. How can You move when there is unbelief?"

from the Lord.

"Go your way, and when you are ready to believe God, come back!"

The onlookers seemed to gasp with disbelief as a hush of anticipation swept the auditorium. The man of faith and power turned away with a clear sense of disgust. His face was beet red with anger and embarrassment. Sweat poured from his forehead as he

The young man also was left behind, there with

The Judgment Is Coming!

walked quickly from the platform, leaving behind dozens of people still waiting for prayer.

his small family. They lowered their heads in shame

and slowly walked back to their seats. The young father's face was beet red with anger and embarrassment. Sweat poured from his forehead as he walked, mumbling with merciless personal chastisement. Relentlessly he rebuked himself for allowing such a spirit to overcome him. He knew better than that, yet he had allowed himself to falter.

The preacher was right. They were trapped in

The Judgment Is Coming!

His wife looked at him with disappointment and pity. She loved him so much, but how would they ever be used of God with such meager faith and barren knowledge of the Word?

weakness. The young mother gathered her children and hugged them tight as she thought of their future with uncertainty and fear.

The preacher nearly ran to his study, where he tossed his Bible onto the couch and threw his arms in the air in total frustration as he paced around the room.

"I have never been so embarrassed! So humiliated!

The Judgment Is Coming!"

"I can't believe it,"

he said angrily to the associates who had followed

him from the podium.

No wonder God's judgment is coming to this country!"

Sweat still poured from his face as he paced the

room in utter rage.

"No wonder He is through with us. I'm telling you, God's judgment is coming. He is through with our unbelief. He is through with our excuses. He's going to judge us— and the sooner the better!"

The room had grown silent. One man seemed to

The Judgment Is Coming!

He tried to speak, but then thought better of it.

This was no time for discussion. Maybe another

time, another place, but certainly not here, and

absolutely not now.

The preacher pointed his finger at his colleagues,

shaking it with firm resolve.

"From now on,"

he spoke with dogged determination,

The *Judgment* is coming!

"I'm going to pray for God's judgment on this country. No more mercy! No more chances. In fact, I can feel it in my innermost being. God is going to judge this nation! He is through with it.

We had our chance and it's all over.

We had two hundred years and we blew it. Our time is up. *The Judgment* is coming and I can't wait to see it happen!"

With a sense of deserved retribution in his heart, the powerful man of God grabbed his coat and walked out.

The fire certainly followed this preacher over the

'The judgment Is Coming.'

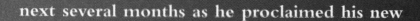

revelation from coast to coast. The airways reverberated

with a message of finality and impending doom.

"There is no hope. God is absolutely finished with this country."

He spoke with eloquent anger as he recounted

the endless failures of the people of God over the

past two centuries, not to mention the Church's

utter refusal to hear what God was trying to say

through him, an anointed and faithful man of God.

From city to city and state to state this prophet

The Judgment Is Coming!

God's patience was exhausted. So when the nation finally refused His word, *The Judgment* was His only recourse.

carried his urgent and deadly message from a God

who was tired of His creation. Other men soon joined in the proclamation, for there were many who shared this man's frustration with the Church and the nation as a whole.

They say adversity makes strange bedfellows. Well, so do frustration and personal offense. Preachers from every denomination and doctrinal persuasion seemed to stampede to join the chorus of voices proclaiming *The Judgment*. Men who would never have been seen together in fellowship were now

Destiny Image Publishers, Inc.

It was a strange collection of spiritual misfits,

'The Judgment Is Coming.'

sharing platforms in a unified declaration of what awaited the land. There was no evidence of disunity here, only a continuous litany of fear and doom. True, it was not the best way to bring men together, but it worked, didn't it?

actually. Each one carried his own baggage of

spiritual and eternal truths.

Some were certain which version of the Bible was correct. Some had cornered the revelation on the Book of Revelation. Others knew better how to take communion. Some spoke in tongues; and some most definitely did not. Some believed in a pre-tribulation rapture; and some, a post-tribulation rapture. Others didn't believe in the rapture; and still others didn't believe in the tribulation. Some believed in only home

kingdom now, kingdom then, or no kingdom at all;

The Judgment Is Coming!

fellowships; and some only the corporate gathering.
Others did not believe in gathering at all.

Issues of grand importance were laid aside: how to
dress; how to baptize; whose name to pray in; whose
church to pray in; how much makeup to wear; who
we should associate with, and who we should not;

Christians in politics; and on and on and on.

How tiresome it all seems. Yet, I guess the vital
importance of these issues to His appearing had to
be most evident to somebody. At least, somebody
much more spiritual than I.

Each personal agenda was vastly different; each
man's stance was normally theologies apart from
those with whom he now joined forces and resources.
The only common thread was *The Judgment*. None of
their particular messages was received and embraced

Shippensburg, PA 17257-0310

It was ironic, really. They all wanted *The Judgment,*

The Judgment Is Coming!

on a grand scale, so their hearts burned in unison with the desire for *The Judgment.*

but each for a different reason. In fact, deep in the

heart of many lingered the belief that some with whom they shared the platform would also be on the receiving end of the very judgment they were jointly proclaiming.

It was quite sacrificial of them, when you think about it. And quite courageous. They were willing to share a platform with others who would be judged, risking their own well-being for the sake of the larger Body of Christ.

Everyone benefited. They all knew just how to

'The Judgment Is Coming!'

But all that is not for us to consider just now.
After all, the most important thing was what unified
them all: *The Judgment.*

seize the opportunity. And seize it they did! Books

were published. Videos were produced. Christian
talk shows were soon buzzing with the news of the
impending catastrophe. What would God do? How
would He judge us? What could we expect? Experts
were called in and very important-sounding analysts
analyzed the situation. Everyone had an opinion;
some even had dates. But all were convinced that
the preacher-man was right.

The response of the average believer was quite
predictable. The populace was utterly devastated.

But the preacher was saying that *The Judgment* was

The Judgment Is Coming!

And why not? They were being told that God had given up on them. This was quite a different notion from being under conviction, from which posture one could most definitely repent.

coming no matter what. There was no more room

for repentance and change. God was fed up with a rebellious humanity and was standing poised to send *The Judgment*. Prayers were useless now; it was to be every man for himself.

Thus began a dark and frightening time as men frantically charted a course to somehow try to escape *The Judgment*. Some tried to flee to another country with their families. They scurried for passports and combed the globe for a suitable destination

Some of these less fortunates looked to buy land in

The Judgment Is Coming!

to raise a family, earn a living, and most importantly, escape *The Judgment.*

But most Christians did not have the financial option to simply "fly away." For them, escape was impossible. They could only try to lessen the impact of *The Judgment.*

remote wilderness areas, some dug shelters under

their homes, and still others installed solar panels or windmills.

Soon an entire industry began to emerge as enterprising speculators began to sell everything from dried food to Geiger counters; from candles to short-wave radios. Such were the actions of a nation that was turning farther from a God who had finally turned on them. All this because of *The Judgment.*

Printed in the U.S.A.

Our man of the hour returned late one night to

The Judgment Is Coming!

It would truly take a miracle now to escape the impending doom. Oh, I forgot, they could not count on that. God had abandoned them.

his hotel room. It had been a grand meeting. More

than a thousand people were now shaking in their boots with terror. But it was good for them. They deserved it. Maybe if they had listened to him a year ago, God would not be planning this. After all, he had spent many years preaching God's love. No one had listened. *Well,* he thought to himself, *they are listening now. But it's too late. **The Judgment** is coming and they deserve whatever God decides to do. No amount of praying will be able to deliver them from this one.*

He did not realize that *The Judgment* he

The Judgment Is Coming!

With that final thought of personal satisfaction, the preacher crawled into bed and fell into a deep sleep. He had no idea what was about to happen to him. He had no thought that the events of the next few hours would rattle his personal faith to the very core of his being.

proclaimed upon an unsuspecting nation was about

to visit him...and it would come with more fury and terror than he could ever have possibly imagined, not to mention preached. I do not think he would have slept so soundly had he realized that he was about to be thrust into a depth of insane horror that would cause him to ask for—no, cry out for—death itself.

The city should have been down there somewhere.

THE JUDGMENT

THE JUDGMENT

Pennsylvania

THE JUDGMENT

New York

California

New Jersey

Florida

?

Place Your Life

Place Your Life

Place Your Life

Pick
A
Card!

The Judgment Is at Hand!

A loud, relentless knocking at the door reverberated through the silent darkness. The preacher jumped to his feet like a lightning bolt had struck him. The room was so dark. He ran to the window. Nothing was there but blackness;

blackness and silence.

But it wasn't. His face knocked against the cold glass

as he tried to reorient himself. The knocking continued. Each knock seemed to shoot a year's supply of adrenaline into his system. His heart raced in terror. His mind raced for answers: Why was it so dark? Where were the lights of the city? And who the heck was pounding on his door?

He stumbled across the room, kicking the trash can and tripping over his own suitcase.

Christian Growth, Inc., Jalan Kilang-Timor, Singapore 0315

His head reached the door long before the rest

THE JUDGMENT

THE JUDGMENT

Pennsylvania

?

THE JUDGMENT

New York

Price Your Life

Price Your Life

New Jersey

California

Price Your Life

Florida

Price Your Life

Pick
A
Card!

The Judgment Is at Hand!

"I'm coming! I'm coming!"

he shouted half in anger and half in confusion.

of him did. Now he tasted blood in his mouth as

he pulled himself up and fumbled for the bolt. Again the knocking. He did not know why he hurried so, for he did not know what awaited him in the hall-way. He tried to look through the peephole in the door, but he could not seem to focus.

His heart still pounding with fear, he took a deep, deep breath and opened the door to a smiling and somewhat bewildered-looking young man dressed with a bow tie and a red jacket.

Omega Distributors, Ponsonby, Auckland, New Zealand

Blood still dripping into his mouth, the preacher

THE JUDGMENT

THE JUDGMENT

Pennsylvania

THE JUDGMENT

New York

Florida

New Jersey

Price Your Life

California

Price Your Life

THE JUDGMENT

Price Your Life

Pick A Card!

The Judgment Is at Hand!

"Evening,"

the young man said with a reluctant smile.

"Room service."

staggered to one side as the server wheeled a cart

into the room.

"Room service?"

the preacher repeated.

"Room service? I never ordered room..."

"Oh, oh yes, you did, my dear sir,"

the server said as he passed in front of the preacher.

He stopped momentarily and wiped the blood from

the preacher's face.

Rhema Ministries Trading, Randburg, South Africa

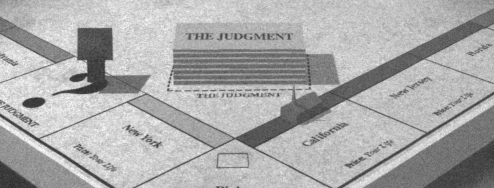

The Judgment Is at Hand!

"Get used to that taste,"

the server said as he walked on by.

"What are you doing here? I didn't order anything."

"Say, haven't I seen you on TV? Aren't you some talk show host or something?"

asked the young server.

Our preacher recovered ever so slightly, long enough to explain who he was, what an important mission he was on, and why he would have been seen on television.

"that He is through with this country and all the

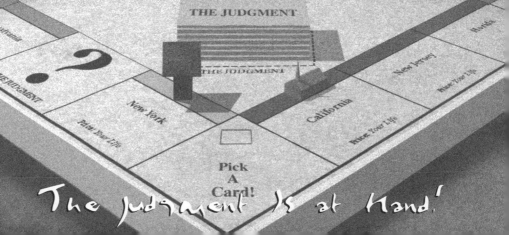

THE JUDGMENT

THE JUDGMENT

Pennsylvania

Florida

THE JUDGMENT

New Jersey

Rule Your Life

New York

California

Pick Your Life

Rule Your Life

Pick A Card!

The Judgment Is at Hand!

"I am surprised you have not heard," the preacher-man said, quite gratified that he was recognized. Then he continued.

"God showed me,"

he started,

Christians. I'm telling everyone about *The Judgment*

that is coming because people will not repent. God has uniquely given me this gifting to speak on His behalf."

The sinister gleam that came into his eyes every time he talked about *The Judgment* was hard to miss.

Our oracle from God was so full of himself that he did not notice the server begin to glow with an unearthly light.

The Angel and the Judgment

'The Judgment Is at Hand'

Successful Christian Living, Capetown, Rep. of South Africa

A sneer of vengeful satisfaction swept his face as he

THE JUDGMENT

THE JUDGMENT

THE JUDGMENT

Pennsylvania

New York

New Jersey

Florida

California

Pick A Card!

The Judgment Is at Hand!

"God has given me opportunities all over the nation to tell people that it is too late. *The Judgment* is definitely coming, so they had better get ready for it."

came from out of nowhere.

"And what would you, O man of God, decree upon such a nation as this, where sin abounds and hearts are hard?"

Startled by the voice, the preacher turned to find that the server was no longer there. In his place was a man, no, a being of enormous strength and beauty.

Vine Christian Centre, Mid Glamorgan, Wales, United Kingdom

Granted, it was not very creative, but at least he could

His voice was full of quiet assurance and his

demeanor was a picture of perfect peace.

"Are...are you from Heaven?"

was all our preacher could say.

say something in the presence of an angel.

"I am an emissary from the Lord on High,"

the angel said.

"The Lord Himself has sent me specifically to you for this occasion. *So I guess,*"

the angel muttered to himself as he scanned his

current assignment,

"congratulations are in order."

WA Buchanan Company, Geebung, Queensland, Australia

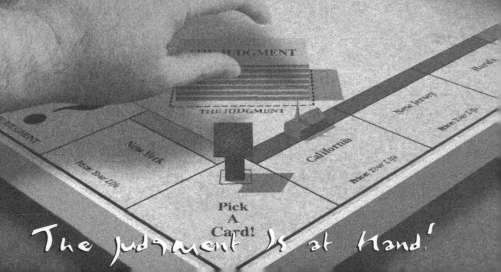

I always thought angels were too busy doing God's

The Judgment Is at Hand!

"Are you sure you are here for me?

for real men of God,"

the preacher asked.

"You have no idea,"

was all the angel said, suddenly getting very serious.

"Anyway,"

the angel continued,

**"you are the one with the message,
so it is all up to you."**

Word Alive, Niverville, Manitoba, Canada

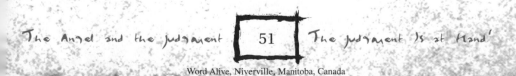

The angel was becoming quite impatient. It was

The Judgment Is at Hand!

"What's up to me?"

the preacher queried rather impatiently.

"Why, *The Judgment*,"

the angel said.

"What judgment?"

the preacher asked, a bit startled by his heavenly visitor's message.

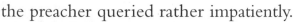

going to be a long night, and he was anxious to get started.

"The Judgment! The Judgment! What? Did you forget already? The Judgment. The thing you are talking about every waking hour. The Judgment on the country,"

the angel responded in utter frustration.

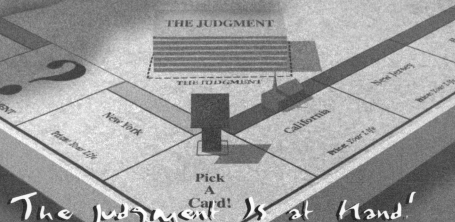

"You sure talk about it enough. So the Lord

The Judgment Is at Hand!

"What do you mean *The Judgment* is up to me? What do I know about judgment?"

asked the preacher.

"Apparently quite a bit,"

the angel responded.

sent me to get your help. I am instructed to

to tell you that whatever judgment you decree will come upon this nation before the end of the year. It is completely up to you. This country's future is in your hands. You may punish it at your leisure."

The angel pulled the only chair in the room directly

in front of the preacher, sat down, and folded his arms.

PESTILENCE
"Come, come now, don't be bashful. There
THE JUDGMENT
THE JUDGMENT
Pennsylvania
THE JUDGMENT
New York
Price: Your Life
California
Price: Your Life
New Jersey
Price: Your Life
Florida
Pick
A
Card!
The Judgment Is at Hand!

"Well?"

the angel coaxed.

Our preacher friend stood rather dumbfounded, so the angel continued to speak.

are plenty of judgments to choose from.

How about a good famine? An earthquake! That might leave a lasting impression. Everyone's expecting California to fall in the Pacific Ocean before too long. Now would be a perfect time!"

But the preacher didn't hear anything beyond God's offer for him to pick *The Judgment*.

PESTILENCE

H

e walked rather aimlessly around the room

THE JUDGMENT

THE JUDGMENT

THE JUDGMENT

Pennsylvania

Pick Your Life

New York

California

New Jersey

Florida

Pick Your Life

Pick Your Life

Pick
A
Card!

The Judgment Is at Hand!

"God wants me to pick
The Judgment.

God wants me to pick
The Judgment?"

as he pondered such an important mission.

"Ah! God wants me to
pick *The Judgment!* He
wants me!"

"That's the spirit, my friend;
that's, ah hum, the spirit. Now,
what shall it be?"

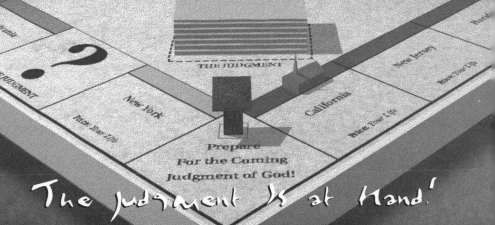

PESTILENCE

The Judgment The Judgment The Judgment

"How shall we bring this nation to her knees

THE JUDGMENT

Prepare
For the Coming
Judgment of God!

The Judgment Is at Hand!

The angel wheeled around to confront the preacher-man face-to-face. His eyes turned to steel and his jaws protruded with gritty resolve.

in repentance?"   "Pestilence."

"What?"

the angel gasped. The preacher had actually caught him a little off guard.

"You heard what I said. Pestilence. I want to judge the nation with pestilence."

The preacher spoke like a man with years of experience.

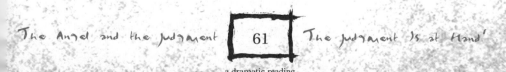

a dramatic reading

PESTILENCE

The Judgment The Judgment The Judgment

"I really beg to challenge your concerns. I have been

THE JUDGMENT

New York

Pennsylvania

New Jersey

Bank

California

THE JUDGMENT

Prepare
For the Coming
Judgment of God!

The Judgment Is at Hand!

The angel responded,

"You don't know what you are asking. You have no idea what this will mean."

The preacher-man interrupted him.

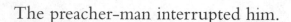

dealing with the likes of these folks all my life and

I tell you, the only thing that will change them is pestilence."

"Then pestilence it will be."

The angel's voice roared like the sound of an inferno as he threw his arms in the air and disappeared in a ball of blinding light and with a noise that sounded like a thousand thunderclaps.

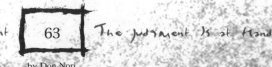

by Don Nori

When the light was gone, so was the angel. Out

The judgment has come!

of the darkness and silence that followed loomed an

eerie sense that something had just happened in the heavens and was about to visit the earth.

As the preacher stood there, the television came blaring to life. He ran to turn down the volume so he could make sense out of what was happening. A newscaster was crying—yes, crying.

with music by John Stevenson

The newsman tried to continue, but the scenes

The Judgment Has Come!

"Scientists are fairly certain that they have finally determined exactly what has happened."

being broadcast were too terrible for words to

describe. The network left him sobbing on a lonely south Florida beach while a stunned anchorman tried to continue from the studio.

"It seems the big storm that blew over Florida last week carried with it an airborne AIDS virus that we suspected existed, but never really saw. The swamps of south Florida apparently acted as an incubator for the virus, which grew faster than anyone suspected was possible.

Death is reported to appear almost painless,

The Judgment Has Come!

"The virus incubated in the swamp and mutated into a form that seems to render it fatal with only one incidental contact with the lungs.

and nearly instantaneous."

Nevertheless, death is death, no matter how painless or instant.

"Yesterday's storm blew the virus north and west in the counter-clockwise movement of air typical in a low pressure system. Nearly half the population of Florida has succumbed to the virus. Scientists estimate that 98 percent of the population will be dead by nightfall."

by calling toll free:

Not even the sight of army blockades trying to keep

The judgment has come!

The preacher stood in silence as the reports continued to come in. He hardly twinged at the pictures
from the Orlando area, where an estimated 40,000
people—men, women, and mostly children—died in
less than one hour.

the people from fleeing northward, away from the

death that crept steadily and relentlessly over the
land, made much of an impression. Nor did it seem
to bother him that the weather satellite tracked the
path of the storm, with its deadly judgment, deep
into the heart of America.

"They deserve it!"

he scowled as he turned off the TV, only to have it
turn on again of its own accord.

In Memphis a shopping mall became an unwilling

The judgment Has come!

Reluctantly the preacher watched as the television, with an apparent mind of its own, moved from channel to channel. Scenes of horror and suffering appeared on each station. In Atlanta a stadium full of sports fans lay forever silent.

sepulcher for hundreds of afternoon shoppers.

In major airports all along the southeastern coast the burning wreckage of hundreds of airliners were smoking testimonies to the merciless carnage. Reports of hundreds of pilots searching frantically for a safe place to land—a place that was both free from the virus and close enough to be reached before they ran out of fuel—filled the airways. Highways also were littered with twisted wreckage as black and angry smoke rolled furiously skyward, marking each spot where yet more victims had met *The Judgment.*

The television continued its slow, almost monotonous

The Judgment Has Come!

running old movies as though oblivious to the carnage outside. One station was apparently abandoned,
except for two anchormen slumped over their desks,
victims of *The Judgment*. A lone TV camera stood
skewed to one side with no operator.

In a surge of triumphant self-righteousness, the
preacher again turned off the TV. Once again, it came
on of its own accord. He then angrily grabbed the
cord of the television, ripped it from the wall, and

For a moment he stood there in silence, but before

The Judgment Has Come!

yanked the other end of the cord victoriously from

the back of the set.

he could feel any relief, the television once again

came blaring to life.

"It's as though it's Judgment Day,"
a nameless voice spoke with chilling finality.

"Government officials continue to tell us that the plague is contained, but these pictures from around the country tell a much different story. These images are live from Washington, D.C."

The pictures moved from city to city as the

announcer detailed the carnage like a sportscaster

announces the evening basketball scores.

The shroud of death rolled without mercy up the

The judgment Has come!

"Philadelphia, Newark, Providence, Hartford, Boston, Bangor..."

eastern seaboard, killing everything in its path.

"California always gets off!"

the preacher shouted with helpless frustration.

"I just can't understand it! If anyone deserves *The Judgment*, Californians do."

He pounded the top of the television with both fists

in anger.

Some FBI agents have confirmed that a new hypothesis

The judgment Has Come!

Suddenly the screen went blank, only to have it reappear moments later with the sound of his own voice gleefully pronouncing *The Judgment.*

"If anyone sees this man, please call your local police. He is wanted for questioning concerning the virus.

is emerging concerning this deadly virus.

Health officials are now saying that there is absolutely no way this virus could have established its deadly course of its own accord. They are speculating that it is a possible act of terrorism by a fringe religious group based somewhere on the East Coast."

Once more the TV abruptly scrolled to another station.

"What was that?"

But he brushed it off with a nervous laugh that didn't

The man of God instantly felt cold and clammy, and his breathing became more rushed. Suddenly, he felt very alone.

Could they really think that I might have had something to do with this? he thought to himself.

really give him any peace.

Meanwhile, the TV blared on from another terror-stricken city as yet another newscaster continued the almost monotonous review of the macabre terror that was now nationwide.

"Airport quarantine efforts seem to have failed. All planes and passengers from the East Coast are being held in hangars for fear of **The Judgment.** *Hundreds have already died there."*

The TV moved mercilessly to another station.

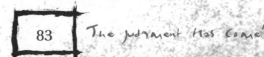

The preacher pounded the television.

"Here in L.A., government officials now speculate that a radical fringe religious element has indeed orchestrated this virus release from the Caribbean."

Another announcer continued,

"Reports coming in from all over the city indicate that this airborne virus was indeed carried to the West Coast and released into the air. Health officials are convinced that it is part of a conspiracy devised by a small religious organization that some say may be a cult. Officials say they need to find the leader to get the antidote.

Unparalleled fear now gripped the preacher.

"If anyone sees this man,"

the preacher was appalled to see his own picture
flashed on nationwide television,

***"please contact local officials. You should con-
sider him armed and very dangerous."***

With a quick move of desperation, he lifted the TV

from its stand and threw it out the fifth-story window, shattering the glass as it fell toward the ground.

He ran to the window and watched it hit the
ground and explode with an unearthly explosion
that rose back up to the window and threw him
against the wall.

Suddenly the angel appeared before him.

Through blurry eyes of semiconsciousness, the
preacher saw the angel's look of deep regret and pity.

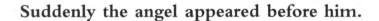

They were after me. I am not the enemy!

"What are you so upset about?"

the oracle of God indignantly asked the angel.

"You've got it all wrong.

I am on God's side, remember?

I am the one pronouncing *The Judgment.*"

The angel stood in silence. There was not much that could be said. Our preacher just did not get it. I guess the angel knew that if he gave the preacher enough rope, he just might...well, let's just say it's best not to engage your mouth when your heart is not connected to your brain.

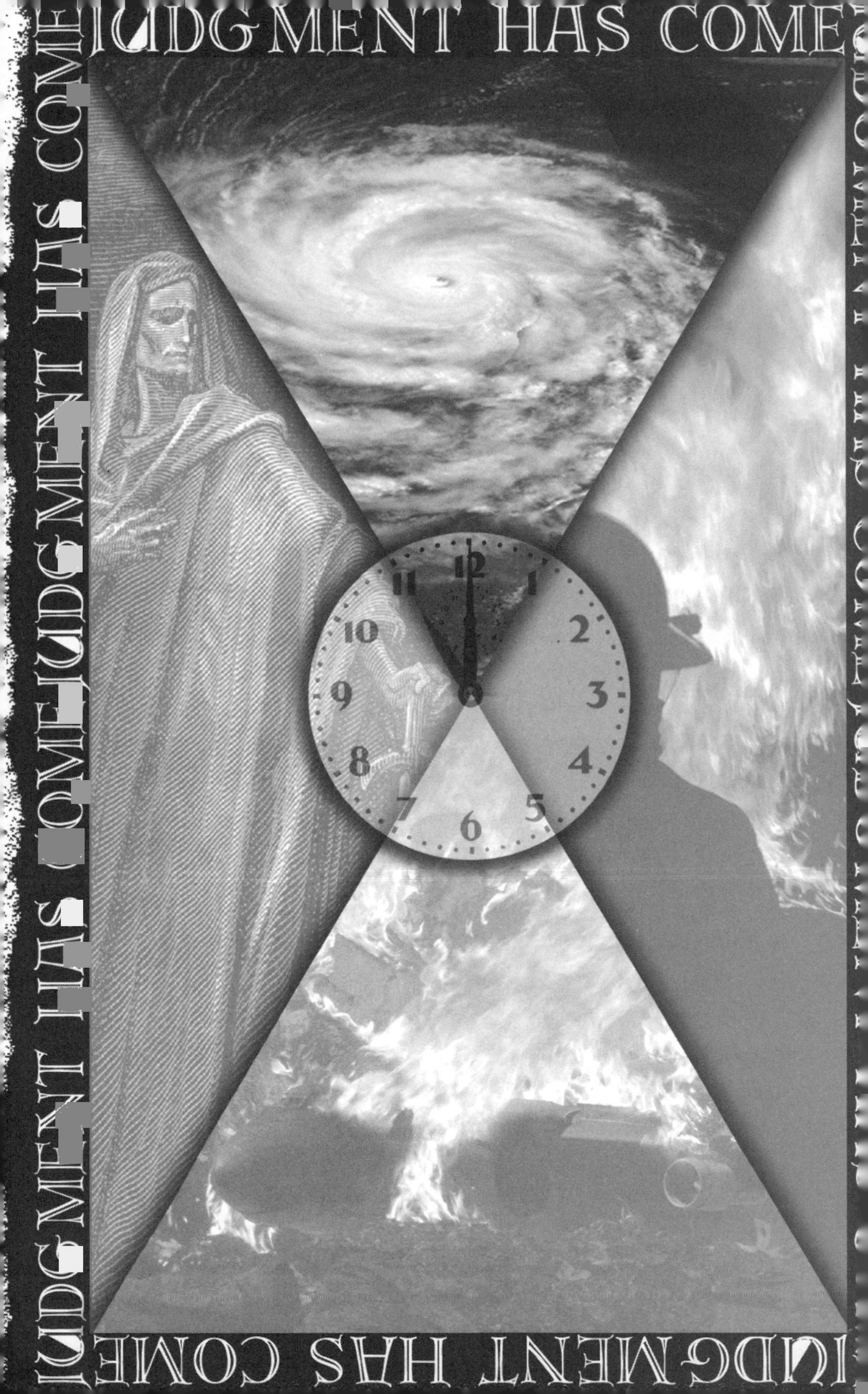
JUDGMENT HAS COME

Then the angel finally spoke.

"You are not going to make this easy, are you? Just remember, it could have been much easier."

"Just what does that mean?" the preacher asked angrily.

But the angel was through speaking. He was not one to argue. Besides, the next event would speak quite plainly to our righteous man of God. With one final look of pity, the angel clapped his hands and disappeared in a splash of blinding light.

"I wonder what that was all about,"

the preacher huffed as he crawled into bed.

"At least that's all over."

JUDGMENT HAS COME
JUDGMENT HAS COME JUDGMENT HAS COME
JUDGMENT HAS COME

The angel was right. The preacher had no idea.

To the preacher, it seemed he had barely closed his eyes when he was rocked by an explosion that threw him far from the comfort of his hotel room, right into the center of *The Judgment* he himself had contrived and orchestrated. There would be no one to blame for this one. He had told the angel he knew better. He was sure that *The Judgment* was the only way. Now he would experience it firsthand.

The stench of burning sulfur filled his nostrils

The Judgment Has Come!

and scorched his already parched throat. He had to

cough, but he could not. He tried to call out

(as if someone was out there to help him), but he

could not. He lay face down in melting pavement,

his cheeks fusing with the macadam as it bubbled

beneath him. He forced his hand into the boiling

tar, pushing himself frantically up so he could roll

to the side of the road.

His clothes ripped from his body as they ignited

in the fiery wind. He rolled over and over until he

reached the relative safety of the roadside, rubbing

He heard nothing. He did not know that the

The Judgment Has Come!

himself in the dirt in a frenzied attempt to put out the fire that covered his body.

He was so riddled with pain that he was not sure he felt anything at all. His hands, now caked with road tar, resembled black bricks rather than hands.

heat had melted his ears closed. But even that was the mercy of God, for it spared him from hearing the sounds of torment and agony from the thousands who surrounded him.

The fireball was too far away for instant death, but too close for him to be spared the torment of *The Judgment.* Nevertheless, fiery confusion engulfed him from every direction. Blackened ruins crumbled as the earth wretched and trembled beneath him. The wind raced across the land, as though itself trying to escape the wicked grips of *The Judgment.*

It was definitely not over. In fact, it had scarcely

The Judgment Has Come!

The troubled earth grew silent beneath him. But
it was a bitter mockery, sending a false sense of
hope and relief racing through his pounding heart.

begun! It was only the beginning of sorrows, and I

am afraid that our preacher would have been quite

content had a large building fallen on him right then.

Alas, not a single large building was left standing to

fall. The land was raped—a flourishing garden turned

into a waste, a howling wilderness, unable to refresh,

heal, or grow again. It was as though, with one final

desperate heave, it fell silent into eternal death.

He was utterly alone. No assistants followed closely

behind him. No one was there to pray for him.

In absolute desperation, he forced in an excruciating

The Judgment Has Come'

There was no one who even knew his name, had he

been recognizable at all.

breath of air. "In the Name of Jesus!" **he bellowed**

loud and hard as he could. Unimaginable pain

ripped through him. His head whirled and pounded

with every word. But all was silent.

"In the Name of Jesus!"

he forced another cry. Nothing seemed to happen.

Absolutely nothing. He was so parched that his cries

could not convince even one tear to fall down his

scarred and reddened face.

He forced himself to breathe, but his lungs

'The Judgment Has Come'

"In the Name of Jesus!"

he cried out one more time before dropping his face

into the punishing grit of that nameless roadside.

resisted the fumes and odors that filled them.

Each breath was a concentrated and excruciating

effort to gasp enough oxygen to stay alive. With each

breath there came a moment of consciousness, but

there was no hope even in that for it brought with it

confusion and a sense of betrayal.

Before long he lay silent, having given in to the real-

ity that he would probably die. So he simply waited on

that nameless roadside for death to have its final laugh.

He lay there with a thousand thoughts—alone,

abandoned, and most assuredly judged.

Blood poured from his face and dripped ever

The Judgment Has Come!

so gently into his mouth. Somehow, he suddenly

remembered the words the angel had spoken an

eternity ago. Yes, now he was used to the taste of

blood, his own blood. *The Judgment* had done it.

The Judgment had defeated him.

For some hideous reason, however, death did not

come. He lay there for what had to have been

hours. Night had fallen, and the only assurance he

had that he was still alive was the horrible stench in

his nostrils...and the pain.

His stomach wretched in piercing agony and his head

The judgment Has come'

The numbing pain seemed to be inside and outside. Every nerve in his body demanded attention as they clamored to deliver protests and pain reports from every part of his dying body.

throbbed in utter delirium. Pain was everywhere,

including a pain lodged deep in his heart.

Suddenly there was a terrifying piercing in his left ear—a piercing as if someone was forcing a large pointed object into the side of his head. He rolled over and over as he cried out in agonizing pain. Finally he came to rest on his back and was shocked to hear the sound of someone talking.

"Room service! Oh, excuse me, sir, but did you order room service?"

The preacher could only groan. He forced his cold,

The judgment has come!

Was he dreaming? Was he dying? Was he hallucinating?

"Oh, never mind, it must be the next body down the road a little,"

and off the angel walked.

macadamized hand out just in time to brush

the angel's leg. The angel stopped abruptly and

turned to the man of faith and power. He stood there

a moment, wondering why a man would not allow

his heart to melt before God. He knew he could

never understand the awesome mysteries of salvation,

but it still saddened him that humanity was so stub-

born and arrogant.

I don't know much, but I do know that it does

The Judgment Has Come!

It is a fearful thing to fall into the hands of an angry God, the angel thought to himself.

not have to be this way.

"Well, so you are alive."

The angel finally broke the silence.

"I wonder how that happened? Everyone within a sixty-mile radius of the explosion was slated to die. *The Judgment*, you know. The rain does certainly fall upon the just and the unjust, does it

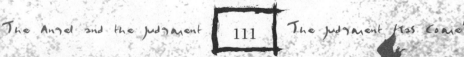

The angel scoured the landscape with his eyes,

The Judgment Has Come!

not? But we do have our quotas. And *The Judgment* does require at least a little pain."

reviewing the countless bodies thrown like

rag dolls over the land.

"Yes. Well, it's these humans, you know. They keep mixing up their own natural feelings with the compassion of God. Something doesn't go their way and all they want is vengeance. 'Call down fire from heaven,' they say.

The angel stopped only momentarily, nudging the

The Judgment Has Come!

'Send *The Judgment*,' they say.
Well, if they only knew what their
lack of faith and rampant human
emotions can cause."

preacher ever so slightly with his foot. The preacher

jerked like a man hit by a lightning bolt and groaned

a deep, quite painful sort of groan.

"Yes, well,"

the angel began again,

**"are you going to stay alive long
enough for the next event? It gets
much more exciting from here."**

The angel pulled a long-stemmed glass of ice water

The judgment has come!

The preacher tried to speak, but his parched throat prevented him.

"What did you say?"

the angel bent over to try to hear him.

"Oh, I'm sorry, you must be desperately thirsty."

from a tray. The soothing moisture both relieved the

man's thirst and restored his damaged voice box enough to talk.

"The next event? You mean there is more? When is this all going to end?"

he whispered as best he could.

"Well, sir, you have no idea how large the mercy of God is. If His mercy prevails, I am sure it will last as long as it has to. God's mercy

The preacher tried to sound confused, but it was a

The Judgment Has Come!

always has your best interest at heart,"

the angel replied.

"What are you talking about?"

meager attempt, for they both knew better.

The angel did not respond.

"Please tell me I am dreaming,"

the preacher whispered.

"Please tell me I am still in the hotel room and this is just a very bad dream."

The angel had an uncanny ability to ignore any question he deemed too ridiculous to answer. This was one of those moments when the whining questions and personal pity parties would not be answered.

"I thought you wanted *The Judgment*. I thought

The Judgment Has Come'

"Does it hurt?"

the angel asked with no pity and only a little sarcasm.

you were praying for it. Your mouth watered

and your heart raced every time you talked about it. You had a gleam of utter satisfaction every time you walked off the platform, leaving the people with no hope and no answers. You loved painting a picture of God that was vengeful and morbid.

You delighted in describing a God whose grace

The Judgment Has Come!

was limited and whose mercy was reserved for

a select few who were just like you. Well, it seems to me that you got what you wanted."

The preacher rolled his eyes in pain.

"Please. Please tell me this isn't happening."

"Okay,"
the angel responded rather offhandedly.

"It isn't happening."

was all the preacher could say as he lay back on the

The judgment Has come!

"Thank God!"

thought he would be transported back to his hotel.

The angel stood silently for a few minutes until the preacher, still in pain, finally looked up with exasperated impatience.

"Are you there, angel?"
he shouted.

"I am standing right here,"
the angel dutifully responded with an honorable salute.

"I suspect it is because less than sixty miles

The Judgment Has Come!

"Why am I still here? Why am I still lying here in such terrible pain?" the preacher moaned.

"Well," the angel began,

away, one of your nasty human weapons of

destruction exploded just a few hours ago and you happened to be in the neighborhood. Excellent timing, if I do say so myself."

"But you said that it really didn't happen," the preacher protested.

"You can't be serious! This can't be real! You must

The Judgment Has Come'

"That was only because you told me to tell you that,"

the angel defended himself.

The preacher lay there in utter disbelief.

make it go away! Take me back to the hotel!"

The preacher's voice was all but gone again as he sobbed. He tried to wipe his eyes with his hands, only to feel the gritty asphalt wrapped permanently around his hands.

"Oh, so now you want it to be a dream? Now you are concerned?"

the angel queried.

"I never thought it would come to me! I never thought

The judgment Has come'

"You were the one preaching *The Judgment*. You were the one who begged God for this to happen," the angel tormented him.

I would be judged. Surely God will have mercy.

Surely there is room in His heart for forgiveness." The preacher spoke desperately to the angel.

"Strange words from a man like you. Strange words indeed. It has been a long time since words of that caliber passed through your lips.

removed these words from His active file.

The Judgment Has Come!

Mercy? Forgiveness? Don't you remember? Your God

They have no meaning now, do they?"

"I don't understand,"
the preacher whined one more time.

"I just don't see why this is happening to me, of all people! Have mercy on me, O God!"

"You have denied God's mercy to the nation, and now you would ask it for yourself as if you have some special exemption?

"Yes, oh yes, His grace would be so grand in an hou

The Judgment Has Come!

Next you will be asking for His grace."

of torment such as this," the preacher interrupted him.

"And precisely where were your prayers for mercy and forgiveness when *The Judgment* fell on others only?"

the angel asked.

"Well, they deserved it."

"And you didn't?"

It was the angel's turn to interrupt.

The preacher was silent, stunned by a view of

The Mercy of God!

notice. There, in the silent torment of his own judg-ment, a miracle began to happen. In a very remote part of his heart, far from his own consciousness, but close to the Spirit of the Lord, an ever-so-small miracle began to happen. His heart began to soften.

The angel waited. He knew the preacher was close. His response in the next few minutes would deter-mine his fate. Life and death hung in the balance.

But the angel raised his hand and held it back.

The Mercy of God!

The Judgment was ready to continue in the preacher's life. The next chapter was waiting to unfold.

Mercy was triumphant as the angel waited for a

response from the man of God.

He watched closely as a single tear began to fall down the preacher's face. As it fell, it washed a streak of soot and sorrow from his face. The man's heart was melting. A little miracle was turning into a major one. The beginnings of a soft heart would soon result in full and utter repentance.

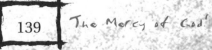

You were called to shepherd the flock. So they

The Mercy of God!

It was time for the angel to speak again.

"A tired and frustrated humanity takes out its pain on an innocent and trusting following.

look to you for hope and encouragement.

They need you to understand their human weaknesses just as Jesus understands the dark night of your soul. You know, those dark and desperate things in your life that you hate and hide because you cannot be free of them. Jesus is able to draw

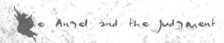

But you didn't care about their pain. You only

The Mercy of God!

these people and love them into repentance because He understands their frailty, as you should, since you too are beset with weaknesses and temptations.

needed their correct response to further your

own agenda. You violated the most sacred trust of the Lord Jesus, who gave you the hearts of His people to nurture and care for."

The preacher wept aloud.

"No, no, I cannot bear to hear anymore. I simply cannot bear it!"

You have already prayed that everyone would

The Mercy of God!

The angel fell to his knees on the ground in near

anger and, grabbing the preacher by the arms,

ignoring the pain he caused, shouted,

"You have no choice in the matter.

know, before they die, the sin for which they

were judged. You have only a few minutes to live and my list is still quite lengthy."

The angel cheated a little. He should not have told

the preacher he was about to die. (It's the mercy

thing again. God's just full of it.) It did, however, help

the preacher to focus again.

"O God, take my life that I might be free from this

The Mercy of God!

The preacher managed to somehow pull himself
away from the angel's grasp as he cried out to God.

torment. Why did I have to survive this holocaust?

Why did I have to live? Take my life, I beg
You. I cannot stand the pain in my body,
and the haunting of my soul is far more
than I can bear."

The angel stood up in silence. This was always
the most exciting part of his missions, for when a
man turns to the Lord, his heart is restored and
people are healed.

JU

flashed by. The sorrow and disappointment they

The Mercy of God!

The preacher could not control the thoughts and memories that now passed through his mind. His ruthless treatment of a family in such serious need suffered pierced his heart like a dagger.

"You are feeling the pain of rejection,"

the angel told him solemnly.

"Not only the pain of this little family but also the pain in the heart of the Lord for your rejection of these little ones. You portrayed a picture of an angry

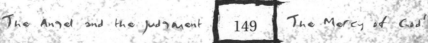

JUDGED

and impatient God just because these hurting

The Mercy of God!

folks did not perform for you.

Their picture of the Lord is now skewed, and their disappointment is about to shipwreck God's plan for their lives."

"No! No! They didn't believe God! They didn't believe His Word!" the preacher defended himself. His heart was melting, but war still raged within him.

JUDGED

"they didn't believe *you*. And they did not

The Mercy of God!

"No,"

the angel responded more gently,

perform for *you*. So you became frightened."

"Preacher-man,"

the angel asked him,

"have you faced the fears and weaknesses within yourself as these precious ones did in front of you and thousands of others that night?"

With every ounce of strength within him, the

The Mercy of God!

preacher forced himself to stand. The pain throbbed

relentlessly through every muscle, and even coursed through his bones.

Tears streamed down his face as he saw the aftermath of *The Judgment* he had pronounced over countless thousands he had been entrusted to care for and pray for. He looked around him and saw thousands of charred and broken bodies scattered over the landscape. He knew it was all because of *The Judgment*.

He saw his own bitterness weaving itself through

The Mercy of God!

the veil of ruthless religiosity. It tangled its way through every relationship and marred everything he had ever hoped to accomplish. The anger that raged in his heart toward himself he had directed toward the weaknesses of others.

He fell to his knees in shame. He groveled on the ground as though to dig a hole large enough to die in. Tears streamed like rivers as he cried out to God. Repentance was actually beginning.

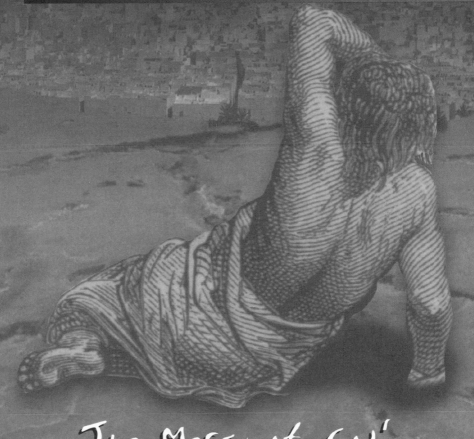

I have sinned to the depths of my very soul.

The Mercy of God!

"Forgive me, O God. Forgive me, O God, if You are able.

If mercy has come to an end, it is my sin that has

exhausted it, not the struggles of Your people. I have mistaken my anger for Your indignation. I have forgotten Your mercy. I have forgotten the pit that You dug me out from. My pride and haughtiness deserve nothing less than death. But please, in Your mercy, grant that these, Your own special treasures, whom I have abused, not suffer for my sin.

"Grant them healing and restoration according to

The Mercy of God!

which I beg, O God, would be inexhaustible. But as for me, I deserve all I am suffering, and I leave myself and my soul in Your all-powerful, all-merciful hands."

The preacher fell face down to the ground. He struggled for consciousness, but could keep hold on it no longer.

HIS

But the server-turned-angel would not release him

The Mercy of God!

The wind blew briskly over the sullen landscape. A damp chill swept the early morning. The preacher struggled for life as the angel of death appeared and demanded that the first angel relinquish the preacher's soul.

and, in a final, glorious act of mercy, the angel of

death was ordered away in a flurry of thunder and wind. The preacher was left lying alone in the early dawn.

The preacher was suddenly startled by a loud knocking. The sound so frightened him that he fell out of bed.

Reaching the door, he fumbled with the bolt while the knocking continued. He finally swung open the door to a curious-looking young man with a familiar smile.

HIS MER

The preacher leaned against the wall, his pajamas

The Mercy of God!

"Room service!"

the young man called.

"It's a new day!"

soaked with sweat. Although utterly exhausted, he

smiled back at the attendant. He knew who the

server really was. He also knew that he indeed had

been given a new day.

The angel rolled the table past the preacher.

"You don't have to dress like that anymore,"

the preacher chuckled.

"After last night, I'll know who you are no matter how you dress."

HIS MERCY I

The Mercy of God!

"I know," said the angel, "but it's easier on the rest of the guests this way. By the way, I took the liberty of calling your secretary this morning. I cancelled all your engagements."

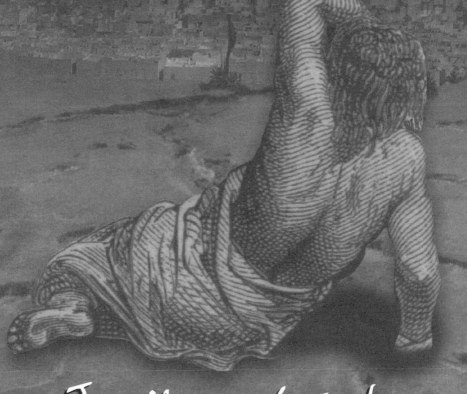

RCY ENDUR

"Oh," the angel continued while he served the

The Mercy of God!

The preacher didn't look surprised.

"Yeah, I don't have the foggiest notion what to talk about now," the preacher confessed.

"I also made an appointment for you to visit a certain family deeply in need of your love and acceptance."

The preacher stood in silence for a moment.

"I guess for a while I have a lot of talking to do outside the pulpit."

NDURES FOI

"True repentance always produces restitution,"

The Mercy of God

the angel responded with resolve and finality.

"You are not going to give me an inch on this, are you?" the preacher asked hopefully.

"Nope!"

The preacher looked at the angel and suddenly grew quite serious.

"If this was all just a vision, then it didn't really happen, did it?

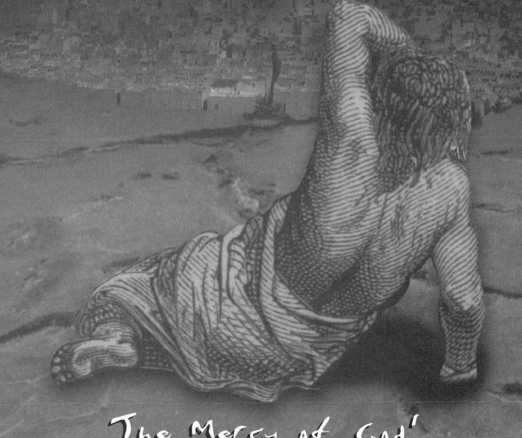

FOREVER

Had I not turned, what would have happened?

The Mercy of God'

"I mean, it wasn't really real, was it? How much of that was real?"

The angel chose his words carefully.

"Let's just say that God works in mysterious ways. Let's just say that the pain in your heart and the angel of death would have prevailed had you not responded to the Lord's plea for repentance. His mercy is boundless."

EVER

Do I need to see a doctor? Is my heart failing?"

'The Mercy of God'

Suddenly a little nervous, the preacher quickly asked,

"What does that mean?

"No, no, no," the angel responded.

"That's the whole point. Your heart is just fine, now."

The angel patted the preacher on the back as he

walked toward the door.

"Make your repentance complete. Go see these young folks, bare your heart, let the Word become flesh in your life right now.

The Mercy of God!

It will be with you then, forever."

The angel continued slowly toward the door.

"I'm probably not going to see you again. I am sure there is someone else waiting to experience God's mercy,"

and he walked out the door.

This time, the preacher's head was not in the

The Mercy of God!

The angel was wrong. He did see the man of God one more time. In a small house in the suburbs, a few nights later, tears of repentance filled the eyes of the preacher once again.

murky loneliness of a distant darkness, but

buried in the shoulder of the young man he had prayed for not long ago.

As husband and wife forgave and prayed, our angel was sent from the Throne with a pitcher of healing balm, which he generously poured over these loving believers. Christ was formed in their midst that night, and a strength was born that would carry their friendship for a lifetime.